Wake Up Do, Lydia Lou!

Julia Donaldson

Illustrated by Karen George

MACMILLAN CHILDREN'S BOOKS

One night a ghost glided into Lydia Lou's bedroom when she was fast asleep.

The ghost said:

Whoo!

Wake up do, Lydia Lou!
Wake from your dream
And scream!

For Poppy and Leo – J.D.

For Lou Bass – K.G.

First published 2013 by Macmillan Children's Books
This edition published 2021 by Macmillan Children's Books
an imprint of Pan Macmillan
The Smithson, 6 Briset Street London EC1M 5NR
Associated companies throughout the world
www.panmacmillan.com

ISBN: 978-1-5290-4253-5

1 3 5 7 9 8 6 4 2

A CIP catalogue record for this book is available from the British Library.

Printed in China.

MIX
Paper from
responsible sources
FSC® C116313
FSC
www.fsc.org

But Lydia Lou didn't wake up.

The ghost tried again.
This time he jumped out and said:

Boo!
Whoo!

Wake up do, Lydia Lou!
Wake from your dream
And scream!

But Lydia Lou went on sleeping.

"I need some help," said the ghost.
So he fetched a kitten.

Mew!

Boo!

Whoo!

Wake up do, Lydia Lou!
Wake from your dream
And scream!

But Lydia Lou just smiled in her sleep.

"I need some more help," said the ghost.
So he fetched a cow.

Moo!
Mew!

Boo!
Whoo?

Wake up do, Lydia Lou!
Wake from your dream
And scream!

Lydia Lou turned onto her back and began to snore.

"I need some more help," said the ghost.
So he fetched an owl.

Too-whit-too-whoo!

moo!

Mew!

Boo!
Whoo!

Wake up do, Lydia Lou!
Wake from your dream
And scream!

But Lydia Lou just
hugged her teddy
a bit tighter.

"I need some more help," said the ghost.
So he fetched a baby.

Boo hoo!
Too-whit-too-whoo!
moo!
Mew!

The teddy looked a tiny
bit scared, but Lydia Lou
just kept on sleeping.

Boo!
Whoo!

Wake up do, Lydia Lou!
Wake from your dream
And scream!

"I need some more help," said the ghost.
So he fetched a cockerel.

Cock-a-doodle-doo!
Boo hoo!
Too-whit-too-whoo!
moo!
Mew!

Boo!
Whoo!

Wake up do, Lydia Lou!
Wake from your dream
And scream!

Lydia Lou slept on,
and a feather floated
out of her pillow.

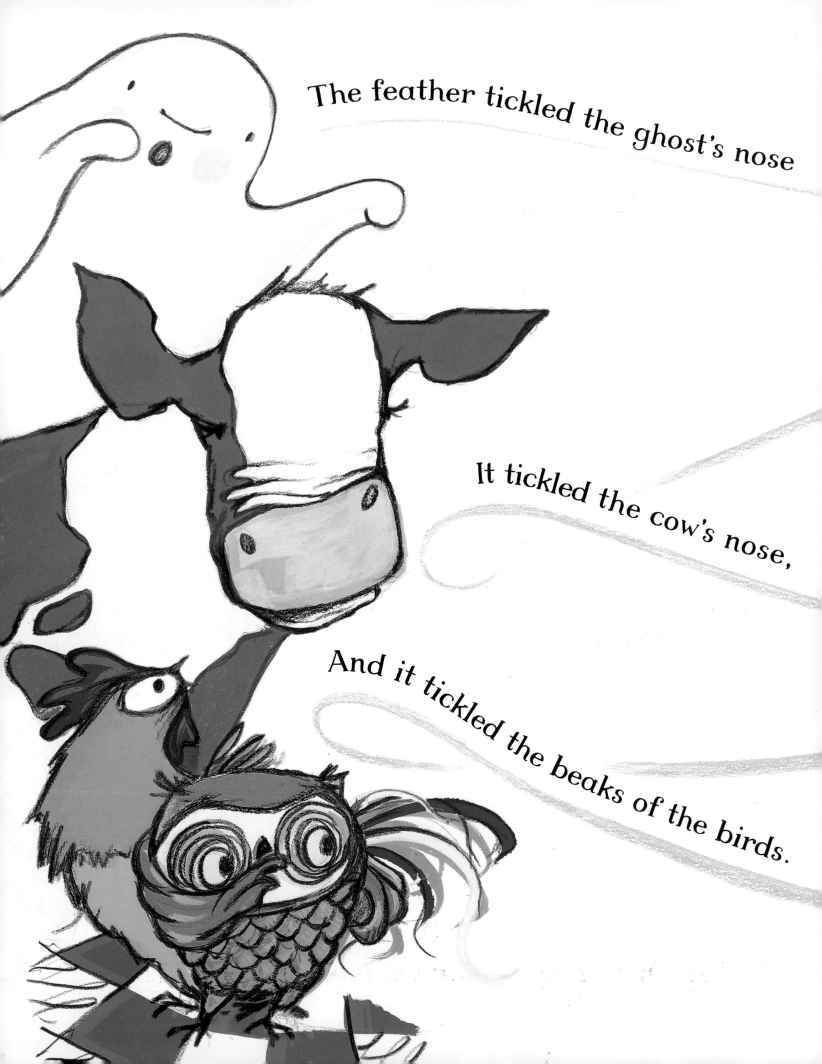

The feather tickled the ghost's nose

It tickled the cow's nose,

And it tickled the beaks of the birds.

and the kitten's nose.

and the baby's nose too.

All together, they let out an enormous sneeze . . .

choooo!

And at last
Lydia Lou woke
from her dream,
and she . . .

. . . laughed!